This Little Tiger book belongs to:

_____

_____

_____

For Bob and Sue
~ N W

LITTLE TIGER PRESS

An imprint of Magi Publications

1 The Coda Centre, 189 Munster Road, London SW6 6AW

www.littletigerpress.com

First published in Great Britain 2005

This edition published 2006

Text and illustrations copyright © Nick Ward 2005

Nick Ward has asserted his right to be identified as the author and illustrator
of this work under the Copyright, Designs and Patents Act, 1988

A CIP catalogue record for this book is available from the British Library

All rights reserved • ISBN 1 84506 203 5

Printed in Singapore by Tien Wah Press Pte.

2 4 6 8 10 9 7 5 3

The BIGGEST BADDEST WOLF

Nick Ward

LITTLE TIGER PRESS
London

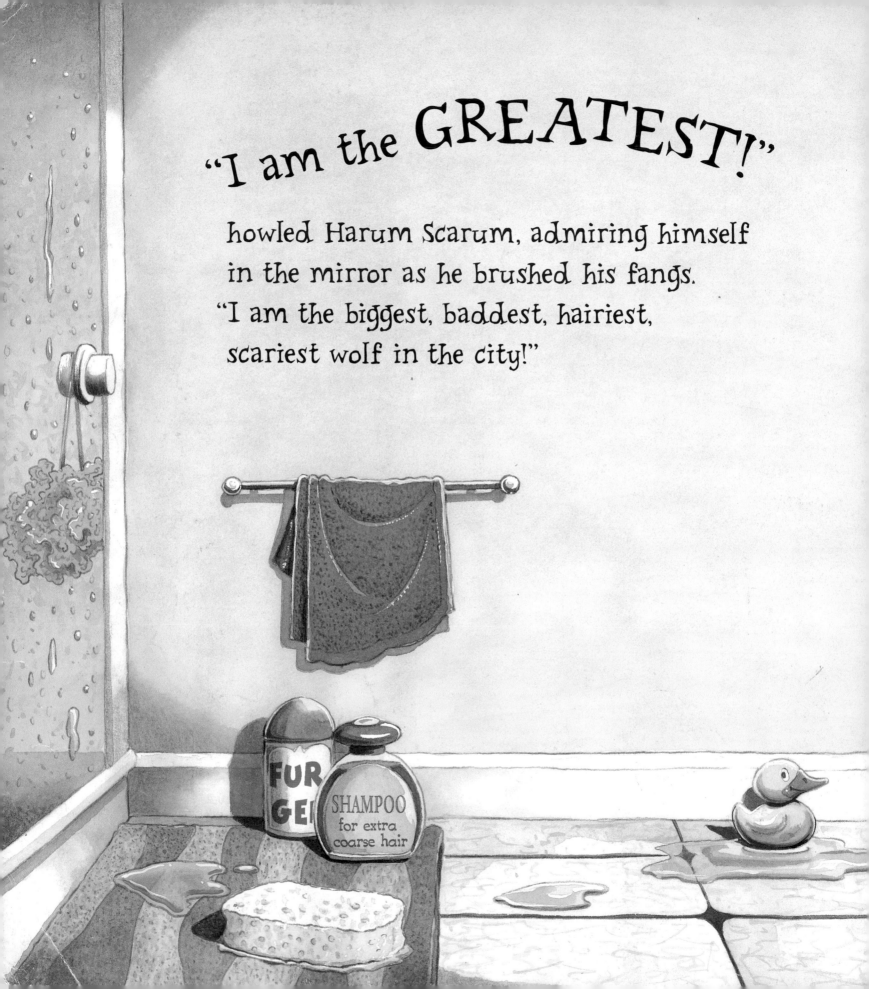

"I am the GREATEST!"

howled Harum Scarum, admiring himself
in the mirror as he brushed his fangs.
"I am the biggest, baddest, hairiest,
scariest wolf in the city!"

Harum Scarum looked at his watch. "Time for some fun," he said.

Harum Scarum's idea of fun was to scare people. Well, he was the biggest, baddest, hairiest, scariest wolf in the city!

"Have I got everything?" he wondered, patting his pockets. "Money, sweets, Teddy . . . Oops, where's my teddy?"

Nobody knew that Harum Scarum had a teddy, and that he couldn't go anywhere without him.

"Ah! There you are!"
he sighed, giving Teddy
a big, wet, wolfy kiss.

He put Teddy in his
back pocket and went
off happily.

First stop was the park where Harum Scarum had some fun scaring all the little children playing on the swings.

"Run, little children, run, or I'll **eat** you up!"

he howled.

"Eeek!" they screamed and rushed away.

"I am the biggest, baddest, hairiest, scariest wolf in the city!" he called after them.

Harum Scarum moved on to the bus stop,
where a group of old people were waiting.

"Run, old people, run,
or I'll eat you up!"

he howled.

"Eeek!" they screamed,
and tottered all the way home.

"I am the biggest, baddest, hairiest, scariest
wolf in the city!" he called after them.

For the rest of the day Harum Scarum worked very hard at scaring anyone he could.

He **startled** a skateboarder . . .

He **petrified** a builder . . .

And he made a street juggler JUMP.

"This is fantastic fun," he cried.

By the time he got home, he was so tired he decided to go straight to bed.

And that's when he discovered . . . he'd lost his teddy!

"Oh no!" he said, frantically searching his room. He looked here and there . . . but he couldn't find Teddy anywhere.

Harum Scarum crawled sadly into bed.
He tossed and turned, but he couldn't
get to sleep without his teddy to cuddle.

The next morning Harum Scarum was a nervous wreck. "I must find my teddy," he wailed, and hurried outside without even brushing his fangs.

He paced the streets.

He searched in every alleyway.

He looked high . . .

and low . . .

But Teddy was nowhere to be seen.

Finally he arrived at the bus stop.
"Excuse me, have you seen a teddy?"
he asked the old people.

But as soon as they saw him they tottered off home shouting, "Help, it's the biggest, baddest, hairiest, scariest wolf in the city!"

Harum Scarum went to the park. "Excuse me ..."
he began, but the little children all rushed off
shouting, "Help, it's the biggest, baddest, hairiest,
scariest wolf in the city!"

Harum Scarum sighed, and a tear rolled down his cheek. But just then he noticed one little boy left playing on his own. And he was playing with ... Harum Scarum's teddy!

"My teddy!" gasped Harum Scarum.

"MY teddy!" said the little boy.
"Finders Keepers."

"Please give him back,"
Harum Scarum whimpered.
"I'm the biggest, baddest,
hairiest, scariest wolf
in the city."

"You don't look so scary to me," said the little boy.

"Please!" cried Harum Scarum. "I'd do anything to get Teddy back."

"Do you promise to do exactly what you're told from now on?" smiled the little boy.

"Of course," he said.

The very next morning, after a good night's sleep, Harum Scarum brushed his fangs and patted his pockets. Whistling happily, he left home and went straight to the park.

"Hurry up," cried the little children. "We're on the swings! Come and push us."

"Coming," smiled Harum Scarum. He trotted up to the children . . .

"Run, little children, run, or I'll eat you up!"

"Eeek!" cried the children, rushing off. "You promised . . ."

"Well, what did you expect?" chuckled Harum Scarum, hugging his teddy. "You should NEVER trust the biggest, baddest, hairiest, scariest wolf in the city!"